THE BOY AND THE FOX

JOEL E. CROSBY

*Dedicated to everyone who
wonders if I'm writing about them.
I am.*

Index

The Boy and The Fox

L ong ago and far away from where most of you call home, there lay a forest, wild and untamed. It sat thick and full and proud, boasting creatures of all kinds, big and small, living in harmony. Among them was a creature far different than the rest. Deep in the woods, in the very tallest tree, there lived a human boy. And it wasn't just any tree: it was a member of the beech family, an oak to be precise. This particular oak had grown to be the tallest tree of the magnificent forest, standing above the treetops that stretched from horizon to horizon. The boy considered this oak, his ever-warm refuge, to be the mother of the forest. It was the largest tree, the one that gave shelter and life to all the creatures within the forest. But it was especially important to the boy.

The boy himself was an enigma to the animals in the forest. Young and spry, he ran through the trees as a child runs through his home, slapping the tree trunks lovingly and drinking from the bountiful streams and brooks. He lived freely in the forest, foraging for food, which was plentiful. The other animals in the forest regarded him with a kind interest, and he regarded them the same way. He did not fear the bears and birds but shared the land with them. He was a thoughtful boy with a kind, quiet demeanor, and each night he would sit at the very top of his tree and watch the sun as it sank below the mountains.

None of the animals knew where the human had come from. Some suspected that he didn't quite know himself. His humanity seemed to diminish the longer that he resided in the forest, but enough remained for him to create a life for himself that was different from the wildlife around him. About six feet from the ground, the trunk of the oak parted into a bouquet of branches that held fenced platforms that the boy had built. On the largest platform—which was near the bottom of the tree—there was a small cabin, just big enough to fit a bed, table, a dresser, and even a wardrobe. The cabin was made of logs; most of the platforms were made of planks and beams of wood. There were even a few small platforms on the smaller trees surrounding the magnificent oak. The roof of the cabin was tall and peaked, made with planks in an overlapping pattern to prevent any rain from seeping through.

The little platforms around the trees that were close to the oak were connected to the bigger platforms around the oak by rope bridges. The boy used the smaller platforms to look out for the deer on their trail to the brook in the clearing.

The forest followed the rhythm of the circle of life, and the boy took part in it all. He built and whistled and worked and sang, wiping the sweat from his brow as the sun beat down upon him. The boy bathed in the river and swam with the fish, who were used to him and did not flee. He fit into the forest like he was born to it.

Some of the animals wondered why he didn't have a home outside of the woods, a home with a family of other silly upright creatures they had heard tell of.

The forest was untamed, unmarred by the heavy hand of man. Its lands were unscathed by blades or bullets, for no human had ever set foot into the shade of its trees... besides this boy. He was, perhaps, the only human in the world who knew of this place. He had lived there for as long as he could remember and it was the only place he had any memory of. It was in his blood; it was his home, just as much as it was home to the deer and squirrels and bears. The boy's thick coconut husk hair and dark green eyes that spoke of the smell of foliage after rainfall revealed the fact that the forest was a part of him just as much as he was a part of it. The forest was his home, and probably always would be. But in truth, it hadn't always been that way.

As all boys do, this boy had a mother and a father, though he could hardly remember their faces. He tried not to remember them at all. He tried, in fact, to scrub any lingering whispers of memory from his mind. Because any time he remembered them, it hurt. Something within him that he couldn't understand would ache, his heart would pound, and his head would become heavy. His nightmares were not about the wilderness. He did not dream of storms or darkness, but of the faces he had left behind. It hurt to remember them. So he did not.

He lived without any family other than his tree, his home, the mother of his beloved forest. And each day, he ran through the woods the way his blood ran through his veins. He thought of his oak as the beating heart of the woods, and he coveted the heart with great pride. The birds that nested there respected him, and he would give them the berries and nuts he foraged when he had eaten his fill. Unlike most men, the boy was not greedy. He took what he needed from the forest, and it provided for him. It gave him all that he desired, nothing more and nothing less. The boy was never hungry, or cold, or sad. Within the woods, he was safe; and though he didn't remember his past, he knew it had not been so secure.

And life in the woods was never boring. The days were filled with work as the boy worked on his cabin and workshop. Eventually, he began to sculpt as well. For hours, he whittled away at wood he collected, creating a menagerie of the animals he saw within the forest. His carvings were beautiful, and though his hands maintained more splinters than he could count, the boy was proud of his work. Some might have gone crazy with such an existence. Some might not have been able to live this way, day in and day out. But the boy knew nothing other than this life, and he was content. He was happy to live his days this way, in the magical serenity of the forest.

There was never a moment where the boy craved the companionship of other people. He was perfectly content to sit in the breeze of the afternoons, listening to the siren song of the leaves rustling. He chewed the sweet honeysuckle and lay beneath the stars, counting them as he drifted off into sleep. There were many nights when he was safe, safe from the memories that tried to creep up on him. And those nights were the blessed ones, the nights he wished to never relinquish. The boy had grown accustomed to his solitary way of life, and he thought, hoped even, that he could continue to live the way he was used to living until his final days. Unfortunately, there came a day when the boy's idyllic life was disturbed.

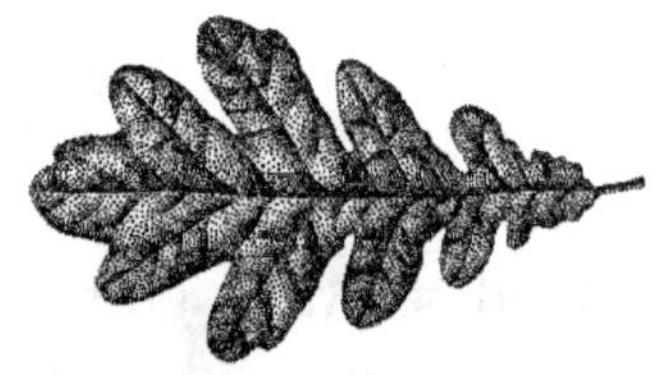

It was raining, though to call it "rain" would be an understatement. Water poured down from the sky like a river. The storm was so rough, it was a miracle the boy's oak remained upright. He had spent many nights in his forest, but none as long as that one. The droplets hammered like hail against the roof of his cabin, and he lay awake on his back, worrying if the structure might give way to the gusting, bellowing storm. Thunder boomed like a terrible song, ringing in the boy's ears as he tried to fall asleep. Normally, when it rained, it was a calming thing. The boy had always liked the sound of rain in the forest, and it lulled him to sleep whenever it came. But not tonight. Something new was on the horizon, brought by the storm. And though the boy had no idea what it was, he could feel it coming in his bones.

Though he recalled little of his past, he always remembered stories of storms, of the way they could bring about change. And this was something that rang true; he had noticed this during his time living within the forest. The boy had seen trees fall, had seen them split from bursts of lumberjack lightning. He had seen fawns born the morning after heavy rain. Though he was not prepared for what would come with this storm, he sensed that something would change.

The morning came with dew and the smell of petrichor, a scent that had always given the boy a sense of melancholy. The way that the soil radiated the scent after rainfall fascinated him. It seemed to produce it so lovingly, so easily. And as he sniffed it, as he listened to the rain dissipate and give way to a drizzle, he could feel a familiar sensation in his heart. The smell made him think about what had been. He thought of rainfalls past, storms that had given way to broken trees and fresh new beginnings.

He hadn't slept at all the night before, so as the rain became ever more gentle and the morning sun peeked into his cabin through the spaces between the logs, he closed his tired eyes and allowed himself the gift of sleep.

As the boy rested, an image stained the back of his eyelids. It was something he couldn't understand, a flash of bright orange that caught his eye, even in the realm of dreams. It left him feeling odd as he awoke in the afternoon, hot from the sun that beat down upon him. The cabin was always hot during the day, at least in the summer months. Stretching and yawning, the boy stood from his bed and walked to the door. He pushed it open and climbed out onto the thick tree branch, squinting at the way the sunlight filtered through the leaves. The day was beautiful, with all the plants vibrant from the rainfall. Two bright-red cardinals sat on the branch above the boy's head, preening.

"Here," The boy held out his hand, emptying a small pouch he had fashioned from deer hide onto his palm. Several seeds fell onto his palm, and the cardinals flew over to land on the boy's arm and feast. He was familiar with these birds. They had raised two sets of eggs on the boy's oak, and he had happily shared his home with the family. As the birds ate, the boy's stomach growled; he was starving, and the rain surely had brought plenty to eat. Once the birds finished their meal the boy slipped down the tree with ease, in quest of something more substantial than seeds.

Effortlessly, he sprang through the trees, enjoying the way that the rainwater fell from the leaves and splashed against his face. He ran towards the watering hole, heart pounding with each footfall, excited at the exercise. This was where most of the fruit trees stood. There was an old apple tree that dropped sweet morsels. Beside it was a lemon tree, and next to that, a peach tree. Behind them, the boy had planted more fruit trees. A blackberry bush sat right on the edge of the water hole, some of its branches dipping right down into the clear water. The boy had become expert at knowing what fruits were ripe and which ones were rotten; he picked himself a generous bushel of apples. He knew that they would last in his cabin, and they were his favorite fruit to indulge in. For the boy, this was candy, the sweetest thing he had ever tasted. He had no concept of treacle tarts and taffy. To him, peaches and apples were appealing enough.

Placing his apples into a sack he had woven from tall, heavy grass, the boy began to walk back towards his cabin. He liked to eat in his home, overlooking the forest and watching to see if there was anything particularly interesting to observe. The deer would sometimes come to investigate, and he would offer them apples if he felt so inclined. They liked the treats and as they ate, the boy and the deer would come to an understanding. He wouldn't hunt them, and they wouldn't fear him. The boy had always lived off of the fruits, vegetables, and fungi that he found throughout the forest. He had no concept of cooking meat, and so he'd never tried, only using the bodies of deer he found already dead to make satchels and clothes.

Quickly, the boy climbed up to his cabin and sat on the platform, looking out across the greens and golds of the forest. Autumn would come soon. He could tell by the way that the leaves were giving way to color. It never became too cold in the forest, and the boy was grateful for this. The heat he could take. It was the cold that bothered him the most. Taking a large bite from one of his apples, the boy allowed its sweet juices to pour down his chin. He opened his ears to the sounds of the forest. The wind blew through the treetops and the birds chirped in the distance. He heard the acorns falling from the trees, hitting branches on their way down, and noticed how lyrical it all sounded. It always seemed to blend into a melody when he started to pay attention.

But today, he noticed something was off, moments before hearing another sound—one that quickly became dominant and drowned out all the other sounds. It sounded as if something was crying out. It was a peculiar sound that he had never heard before in the forest.

The boy climbed further up into the oak and looked out over the trees, squinting to try and see what might have been making such a noise. In the distance, he saw a flash of orange that caught his eye and held his gaze, but it disappeared. He peered out further, trying to see if he might be able to recapture the thing in his eyesight. But it was gone, and he was left feeling confused, and rather dazed. He was usually so in tune with everything in the forest, and he had no idea what he had heard or seen.

While his mind was flooded with questions that might be forever left unanswered, he returned to his cabin and placed his bow and quiver back in the hollow log where he always kept them. His heart, he realized, was beating hard in his chest, and he wanted to calm it desperately, knowing that he shouldn't have such fear. But something had awoken within him, an odd feeling of dread he could not contain. There was one thing that he always did to calm his nerves. The boy went to his workbench and grabbed a piece of dried wood the size of his fist. He had been curing it for weeks, ensuring that it was fine to be carved. If not done correctly, the wood would splinter and his work would shatter, leaving nothing behind but mess and pain. The boy took his stone knife from its place on the workbench and began carving and shaping the wood. While normally he did that for entertainment, this time it seemed he was doing it to bring a halt to these unanswered questions flooding his mind. It worked; his fingers worked deftly around the wood, and he found himself so engrossed in the work that he didn't even realize that the sun had gone down. His eyes were beginning to grow heavy.

The next day the boy awoke still seated at his workbench, his knife dangling from his right hand and an unfinished animal sculpture in his left. It was already taking shape, and the boy groggily placed it carefully down on the bench. Immediately a quick flash of yesterday's events, that spark of reddish-orange, shot through his mind. Sculpting hadn't helped to drown out the unanswered questions after all.

What could it have been? he thought to himself. The boy sat on the ground with his knees to his chest and his back against the wall. A burning sensation began to form in his throat and his eyes were welling up with hot, heavy tears. He had no idea why he had this sudden emotional reaction, but it was as though there was something within him warning him. Something telling him that his life was about to change.

The boy had been alone for so long that he had grown accustomed to his solitary way of life. It was consistent, and that had always given him comfort. He had started to believe he would be alone forever.

While thoughts rushed through his mind, he had brought his hands against his ears. He didn't want to hear any sounds and he didn't want to hear his thoughts. But he couldn't stop thinking. The boy wept at the realization that he wasn't alone and the fear that came with it. He pulled his knees up to his chest and sobbed into them, wishing for comfort that he knew he could not get. For the first time in a long while, he wanted to feel the touch of a mother, of a father, to comfort him and tell him everything would be all right. He saw the way that the deer nuzzled their young, saw how the birds encouraged their hatchlings to fly, and suddenly he wanted that. The boy couldn't tell if he wanted to be alone, or if he was suddenly frightened by being alone.

Shortly after he wiped the tears from under his eyes, the boy grabbed his bow and quiver and left his oak, determined to find the thing that he had seen in the forest. Resolutely, he scurried down his tree, looking intently down at the path below. It was expansive, and he followed it, looking at a strange set of prints with a keen eye. He had learned to track creatures when he taught himself to hunt deer, and so he knew how best to follow the animals. And find where they had come from. But the prints themselves looked odd. They were small, and looked like a cross between some kind of cat and some kind of wolf. The boy wondered what they could possibly belong to.

His journey took him through a large part of the forest he knew well. There were places in the forest where a lot of oaks grew; one of them was where the boy's oak stood. Then there were areas with a lot of maple trees, all clustered together. The maples gave off a sweet scent that the boy found cloying; he much preferred his oaks. In one large part of the forest, there were a lot of chestnut trees and pine trees as well. They all bowed to the wind and shed their leaves and needles. The boy had taken pine needles and used them to make his bed. They were comfortable, and their scent kept large bugs from infesting his home. Less common were trees such as yew trees from which one could make perfect bows. The boy had taught himself to whittle such bows from the yew trees and was always careful not to exhaust his resources. After all, there was only so much he could take.

Apart from being a thick forest, it was also very hilly. The hills increased the further he went from his oak, making his legs ache the more he went uphill. Though he was strong, with legs sinewy from years of running and climbing, his long journey exhausted him.

The uneven terrain, full of sharp rocks and edges, scraped at his calloused feet.

The boy halted at an open space at the edge of the forest. This was the farthest he had ever gone, and the thought made his heart drop into his stomach as he looked beyond to unfamiliar lands. He was tempted to look back, to see his home from this distant place, even though he knew it would terrify him to see how far he was from his oak. He decided against it and kept moving forward. The forest was expansive, far larger than anyone might suspect from looking at it from afar. The trees kept the boy cool as he journeyed on through the midday heat, and he was grateful for their cover.

Ahead were the mountains the boy had always called "rocky hills." He passed under a stone arch as he walked along the mountainside. There the boy realized that it would soon be nightfall, and felt a shift in the wind as the humidity rose. Another storm was about to hit. His heartbeat quickened, and he decided it was time to make a split decision. If he stopped tracking the paw prints now, they would be washed away by the rain. But if he stayed out and weathered the storm, he might be injured, or worse. And it would be difficult—though not impossible—to find his way back to the tree once night had fallen.

He began walking at a faster pace, hoping he would find shelter in the mountains before rainfall, but the wind started picking up and whipped against him, causing him to turn and run back towards home. He was fast, and gracefully jumped and moved over the land with the agility of an animal that knew its home. He sensed the storm as it came, felt the electricity charging the air. The black clouds were beginning to give way to fat, cold drops of water, and they pelted the boy's face as he ran. As he neared his oak, he wondered: *What would come from this storm?*

Several more weeks passed without incident. The boy didn't see any more strange things passing through the woods, and as time marched on, he began to forget about the curious flash of orange. It was easy for him to take up his routine again, and he fell back into it happily. Though seeing the thing had perturbed him, he wanted nothing more than to get back to his life, the life he loved so much.

The boy spent the rest of the day scavenging for food around the familiar areas of the forest that he knew had food. He collected apples, peaches, and plums in his bag, as well as several carrots and herbs. He knew the places where the edible fungi grew, having watched the deer day after day as they guided him towards the things that were safe to eat. He continued to forage, collecting some sprouts and wild spinach before heading to the water hole. He had learned to always wash his plants before eating them after he had dealt with a particularly bad case of the stomach flu. He brought his clean food back to the cabin and feasted, enjoying the raw, fresh fruits and vegetables. After his meal was finished, the boy gathered the rest of the produce. It was more than he could eat right now, and he didn't want it to spoil. He brought it down to the base of the tree, and left it there as an offering for the deer. They would eat it during the night; that was how it always worked. As he climbed back up, he smelled the familiar scent that alerted him that a storm was brewing in the distance. Just as the thunder was beginning to echo across the sky, he went to his cabin. Heavy rain could drip through the small spaces between the logs, but it never bothered him. And anytime the wood would rot, he would never have any trouble replacing it. That was one of the perks of living in a forest.

He lay on his back, staring at the ceiling of the cabin, listening as the storm raged on outside. As he gazed up, he wondered what damage he might wake up to in the morning. He felt no desire to fix anything that the storm might break today. But he knew it was necessary for him to continue to survive.

The next morning he awoke to a post-storm home. Though he had avoided damage in the past, this time his home had not escaped unharmed. The roof was beginning to break off, and one of the logs from the foundation of the cabin was slipping out of formation. The boy inspected it and saw that it was rotting. Sighing, he began to head out to the woods, stone knife in hand, to salvage another log to repair the house. He climbed down the tree, his bare feet hitting the mud of the ground with a small squelch. The boy grimaced, making a note in his head to bathe after he finished repairing his home. As he walked out into the woods, he thought he heard a strange sound coming from beyond the oak trees. The boy listened intently, trying to determine what the sound was. Ever since the strange tracks he saw, and sounds he heard, he had been on edge. But when no other sounds grabbed his attention, he continued, shifting the deer-hide bag he had crafted to his other shoulder.

It wasn't until he got to another tree, and was ready to chop into it, that he heard the strange sound again. It was the sound of an animal crying, almost screaming. The boy recognized it was the sound of something in pain. He listened for another moment, unsure of what he should do. Finally, he decided he should investigate. Placing his knife back into the bag, he followed the sound of the cry. It became louder, then soft again, then silent. Then it grew loud again. The boy realized that the animal was likely in so much pain that it needed to rest before each cry for help.

He finally saw it lying in a patch of grass, its brilliant orange fur tainted with sticky, red liquid. He gasped as he realized what he was seeing. This thing was the flash of orange he'd spotted the other day. It was a small fox, a beautiful creature, and as it lay there, taking labored breaths, the boy couldn't help but feel sorry for it. He leaned over the animal and took it gingerly into his hands. It was covered in mud and dirt and blood, and a foul smell came from its fur. The boy cradled it to his chest, realizing that it had stopped crying and was now whimpering softly against him. It was hard for his heart not to swell as the animal nuzzled into him.

At the water hole, the boy gently placed the fox down at the water's edge. He took his hands, cupped them, and brought a small amount of water up to the fox's face. The animal lapped it up greedily, as though it hadn't been able to drink anything for a long while. The boy watched it, considering. He wondered what the creature had been through. The storm had been bad, but he didn't think the weather could have injured the creature so badly.

The fox drank more, still weak, eyes closed. It was female, and its body was the most vibrant shade of orange that the boy had ever seen. She reminded him of a gorgeous, flittering cardinal, delicate and bright. The eyes of the fox opened slowly, and he saw that they were a piercing blue, a cold ice that held him as he looked into them. They were trained on him in a way that made him feel as though she knew far too much about him. But she was still injured and still unkempt, so he carried her gently into the water. He bathed her, as he bathed himself, and watched as the water ran red, then brown, then pink, then finally clear. He carried her from the water, cradling her small body. The fox was drowsing, comforted by the warmth of his arms. The boy wondered sadly if she would live through the night.

He brought her up to his cabin and laid her on his bed. She slept all through the night, and he kept his hand against her rib cage, just to make sure that her heart was still beating. As the sunlight filtered in the next morning, he watched while her eyes opened, and she surveyed her surroundings, looking more intrigued than scared.

"Where am I?" she asked, her voice small and polite.

"My home," he answered quietly. "You were hurt."

"Yes," was all she said. It was a simple response, giving no added detail, offering no thanks for him saving her. He sat back on the bed and watched as she stretched and leaped onto the floor, inspecting her surroundings. Her nose twitched as she did so, and he couldn't help but smile at her curiosity. The fox continued to explore his tree, and when he went to sit at his workbench and continued to carve his latest piece, she followed.

"What's your name?" she asked, her head tilted inquisitively. He looked at her questioning azure eyes that seemed to want to know everything at once.

"No one ever gave me one," he replied, continuing to work on his carving. He had never thought of himself in any capacity. No animals had ever asked for a name. They had perhaps given him a name in their minds, in their circles. But for him, it was as unnecessary as naming the wind or the sea.

"Well then, what do you call yourself?" she responded, pressing for an answer.

"I don't call myself anything," he stated. "I have no one to talk to anyway." Which was the truth. Even when he was alone, talking to himself as he worked, he referred to himself merely as "I," and nothing more. He didn't remember what his parents had called him. Just thinking about the subject of a name made his stomach churn.

"Then what should I call you?" was her immediate reply.

"That's up to you," he decided. After all, it didn't matter to him in any way. "Whatever you like." The boy shrugged, whittling away at his sculpture. "And what about you? Do you have a name? A family?" He glanced at the fox, who looked as though she hadn't been expecting him to ask such a question.

"You can simply call me Fox," she said, shifting her blue eyes away from the boy, "And I did have a family, but I left them behind." Her paws were folded delicately in front of her. The boy noticed how her body language had changed.

"Why did you run?" he asked, raising his eyebrows at her.

"They weren't kind to me," she answered, carefully. The fox tilted her head, considering. "Though perhaps I was too hasty with my judgment." Though her words said one thing, her uneasy tone said another.

"Perhaps I should take you back to them. They must be worried sick," the boy said. The fox seemed to frown, thinking for a moment.

"Can we be friends?" she asked the boy, and he nodded, unsure of what the implications of having a friend were. "Thank you, by the way. Thank you for saving me." She gave a small smile, and he smiled back at her. It was the first time he had shared a smile with anyone.

"Are you cold?" he asked, noticing that she trembled slightly.

"Only a bit," she shook her head. "Should we make a fire?"

"A what?" the boy asked, raising his eyebrows. He had never heard of such a thing before, but the word seemed to cause unease within him. The word *fire* gave him pause and made his stomach turn. There was something about it that bothered him, though he wasn't sure what it was. Part of him was afraid of it. But the fox ignored his inquiring tone and set to work creating a fire with some of the scrap wood in the shop. She was very quick about it, and soon she had created a pretty, warm, constantly moving thing that lit up the room. This small, orange, flickering creature wasn't frightening at all. Rather, it was an inviting, lovely thing that made him feel comfortable. As he drew nearer to it, holding out his hands to warm them, he noticed that it made his body feel less pained. There were fewer aches within him as he got closer.

"See?" the fox crooned, and the boy nodded, feeling silly for ever having been afraid. "And it's not just for warmth."

"What else can you use it for?" the boy asked, looking at her with great interest. This fire was so fascinating, like a toy that he was still learning about.

"Have you ever eaten deer meat?" she asked, smiling slyly. The boy shook his head.

"I only eat the things that grow in the forest," he said. "Fruits and mushrooms and leaves."

"You can cook yourself some meat with the fire. And it tastes delicious." He thought for a moment about the dead deer he would occasionally find in the forest. Up until now, he had only ever used their skin, but he wondered what the meat might taste like. The fox allowed the fire to burn a little longer before snuffing it out with the clay jug of water the boy had in the room. She stayed the following evening with the boy.

The next morning, the boy and the fox ventured out into the forest. He had told her that it was time to find her family, and she had agreed, though her face was serious. In the little time the two had spent together, she had started to cling to him, wanting to be near him all the time. She snuggled into his chest as he carried her, and her body was almost unbearably warm in the heat of the day. And though she was reluctant to go back to her parents, she eventually told the boy how to get to the hollow in which she lived.

They didn't have to travel far, which the boy was grateful for. He was sore from repairing the house, and caring for his new friend had also taken a toll. The boy was not used to caring for anyone but himself. Of course, there were times when he shared his food with the deer, but other than that, he had been self-sufficient. And it had been a good life, being alone. He didn't have any deep feelings for the little fox, even as she stayed nuzzled so close to him. If anything, he felt slightly perturbed by her intense attachment.

"We're here," she said, peering at a small clearing where two sheep grazed. The boy hesitated as they drew closer. The sheep looked strange, though not nearly as malicious as the fox had made them seem. She had told him that they were more like wolves. But as the boy looked upon them, he saw they were nothing more than sheep. "These are your parents?" He whispered, and the fox nodded, her claws still digging into the boy's shoulder. The sheep both raised their heads, and before the boy knew what was happening, they were rushing towards him and the fox.

"We were worried sick," the male said severely. The female nodded in silent agreement.

"I'm okay," the fox said—though she looked downright miserable. The boy wasn't sure why, but he had a sudden desire to take her away from the strange-looking sheep. He couldn't put his finger on why. Perhaps it was the way that she skirted her gaze away from them. He wanted to protect her from everything, even if it meant it made him uncomfortable.

"Please, put her down," the fox's father commanded. The boy did as he was told, unhooking the fox's claws from his deerskin tunic. She was reluctant as he placed her before her parents.

"Thank you for bringing her home to us," the father said, leaning down to nuzzle the fox. But she moved slightly, keeping out of his reach. The boy watched uneasily. He didn't want to take her home again, but she seemed so uncomfortable around the sheep. How could he, in good conscience, leave her with them?

"I don't want to be here," the fox muttered, both to her parents and the boy. Her mother looked rather hurt, and the boy felt a bit surprised that she would say this in front of the sheep.

"Where would you like to be?" asked the father, gently. The boy was beginning to see that, though he and his mate were a bit odd, they didn't seem malicious in the slightest.

"I want to go home with him," she walked back towards the boy and nuzzled his leg with her nose. He wanted to move away from her, be done with her, but instead, he found himself picking her up once again. She wouldn't allow herself to be put down again. The boy decided, as storm clouds began to roll in, that it was better to take her home than to risk her running away and into danger once more.

Her parents reluctantly agreed, and as the storm made its way into the forest, he ran back to the cabin.

Once again, thunder began to echo across the skies, and rain started to fall as they hurried home. He climbed up quickly, still grasping the fox for dear life, and jumped into the cabin, out of the cold rain. They were both soaked to the bone, and the boy stripped out of his tunic and lay on the bed, panting. The fox shook herself off and curled up, shivering.

"Fire," she said, her voice trembling. "We need a fire."

"Why didn't you want to stay with them?" he asked, looking at her as she shook from the cold.

"They're monstrous," she replied, but offered no further explanation. The boy sat for a moment, not fully understanding why she hated her parents so. But if she needed to be protected, he would do what he had to in order to make her happy and safe. Even if it caused him discomfort. She was his new obligation, a responsibility he didn't want, but knew he had to take on.

"Maybe we can find you a new family," he suggested.

"You can be my family," the fox said, but the boy didn't answer. Instead, he stood and walked towards his pile of dried wood. He remembered how the fox had done it, and he began to rub the wood together vigorously, blowing on it from time to time. It took him far longer than it had taken her, but he soon had a small flame that grew the more wood he put on it. The fox huddled closer to him, resting her chin on his lap. They sat there, with the flames growing larger and hotter. The boy moved back, starting to feel a bit nervous. It was giving him warmth, yes, but the warmth was beginning to get uncomfortable, and smoke was beginning to fill the small cabin, hurting his lungs. He coughed, and the fox looked up at him. "Are you okay?"

"I think we need to kill it." He looked at the fire, and the fox laughed dismissively.

"No, no, we need it so we can stay warm," she said, but he wasn't so sure. It seemed that the fire was a creature with a mind of its own, and it was beginning to grow even bigger. It was spreading through the cabin now, licking at the walls in a way that was beginning to truly frighten the boy. He stood fast and grabbed his clay pitcher, throwing water onto the fire. But it wasn't enough to put it out. Gritting his teeth, feeling his heart about to leap out of his chest, he grabbed his last pitcher and threw the water at the fire. As he did, it began to die down. Instinctively, the boy grabbed his still-wet tunic and began beating the fire with it.

The orange flames finally sputtered out, leaving a smoldering heap of ash in their place. The boy looked at it, breathing heavily. He could feel the fox's eyes on him, and he glanced at her. She seemed unperturbed by the events, and yawned, closing her eyes as she curled up and fell asleep. The boy sank onto his bed. He had liked the fire at first. But now, as he stared at the blackened spot, he was afraid. It had almost gotten out of control. His cabin, his oak tree, his home, and his life, had all been at risk. Shaking his head, he decided he wouldn't make a fire again.

Though the boy hadn't intended for the fox to stay any longer than she already had, she made herself at home in the cabin, and in his life. She consumed him in a way that no other creature could, and at first, he didn't understand it at all. He didn't think that she was doing it on purpose, but she had dug her claws into him in such a way that he was stuck with her. And she wasn't easy to please.

The boy's days full of freedom and fun were over; he spent most of his time taking care of her every whim. She had trouble sleeping and begged him to stay with her during the day. Whenever he wanted to run and explore the forest he loved so deeply, she would cry and claim he didn't care for her. And the boy did care for her, enough to make more sacrifices than he had ever made for anyone. His days of sculpting came to an end; she didn't like for him to have hobbies that didn't involve her. If she needed a shoulder to cry on, his was the only one that she could accept. And she would make him lie beside her, even in the daytime, just so that she could rest her snout on his chest and hold him there, her protective hero.

But as she was becoming happier and happier with the arrangement, the boy was becoming more distraught. She was turning him into something he didn't want to be. He was constantly under her watchful eye, unable to do the things he liked. His life was becoming more and more miserable, and she became ever more controlling. Eventually, one evening, things came to a head.

It was a cold evening, and the two had just gotten back to the cabin after an afternoon of foraging together. The boy didn't like bringing the fox out when he went to look for food; she slowed him down considerably. But she would cry and moan and threaten to jump from the tree and fall to her death if he didn't take her. So he did.

On this particular evening, he had found a great harvest of hazelnuts, which were a special treat for him. Hazelnuts were his favorite food, and it was rare that he was able to find so many. As they walked back into the cabin, he was elated, looking forward to the rare treat. He fixed the fox's meal, arranging it on a small, clay plate, before taking out his prize and cracking into them. The fox stopped eating and watched him, her eyes suddenly steely.

"What is it?" the boy asked, popping a hazelnut into his mouth and enjoying the creamy, woody taste. The fox gave him a reproachful look.

"I don't like the face you make when you eat those," she said, and he laughed, thinking she was joking.

"What do you mean?" he asked as he noticed that her face stayed stony. She sniffed haughtily and walked over to the bag of hazelnuts, picking them up in her mouth and bringing them to the door of the cabin. He watched, bewildered, as she threw the nuts to the ground far below. The boy could hear them scattering as they fell, and knew he wouldn't get to them before they were taken by squirrels. "Why would you do that?" he asked, genuinely perplexed. He wanted to be angry, but he was more sad and confused. After all, the boy had given the fox everything. And this was how she treated him?

"You look too pensive when you eat those. Angry. And I don't like it," she said simply, laying down and languidly finishing off the food in her own dish.

"That isn't fair," said the boy, frowning. "Those were mine and I was enjoying them. Hazelnuts are my favorite."

"I don't want you eating them around me." The fox spoke with a finality that told him the conversation was over. But the boy didn't like this.

"But that's not right. I should be able to choose what I eat," he said gently, not wanting to set her off. But it was too late. He knew what was coming before it even came out of her mouth.

"So I guess my feelings don't matter to you. You hate me, don't you? I should just jump from the tallest branch to my death, is that it? Or perhaps I can poison myself, I'm sure you'd love that." The boy sighed as he looked at the fox's shining eyes. He didn't know how to comfort her, and he wondered why she was the one who needed to be comforted when he was the one who was hurting. He shook his head and turned his eyes to his bowl of greens, which he finished quickly. As evening fell, the boy lay down and went to sleep, his heart heavy.

The next day, as the sun peered through the trees, awakening the boy and the fox, he decided that it was time for him to find her a new family. She was too much, and he didn't think that it was a good idea for her to live with him. Though when he tried to tell her, she had turned her eyes downward, looking pitiful.

"I'm sorry," he said to her, feeling guilty. After all, she had nowhere to go. "I just don't think it's smart for us to live together. You need your own family. And I like to live alone."

"But I feel happiest when I'm with you," she whined, cuddling up to him. He wanted to pull back, but he couldn't help feeling sorry for her. He didn't care for her the way she cared for him; her feelings for him had become more of an obsession. He couldn't leave the cabin without her wanting to tag along. The fox wanted to be with him at all times, and she would become sad or sometimes even angry when he wouldn't allow her to be with him. It was tiring, and he knew that the most important thing was to find her a family. "I don't want to be with anyone else," she said plaintively. "And you need someone to light the fires. I know it made you nervous last time, but you need to be able to have them in here. To stay warm and comfortable."

"It got out of control last time," the boy said sternly. "I don't want that to happen again. Who knows what can happen?"

"You worry too much," The fox sniffed, looking rather angry. She had an air of arrogance to her sometimes that suggested she thought she knew what was best for the boy, even in his own home. He tried not to take offense, even as she clung to his side.

He allowed her to stay another night and didn't complain even when she climbed into his bed and lay on his chest. She dug her claws into his skin, and he didn't push her off, for fear that she might rip his flesh. But it still hurt to have her hooks in him, in more ways than one. He had never felt trapped before while living in the forest, but suddenly, this small fox, this animal he had chosen to help, was keeping him on a leash. Soon, one more night turned into another.

Then another. And suddenly, she was there for more days than the boy could keep track of.

"I don't want to leave you, not ever," she said one evening when he suggested again that he help her find another family. Her eyes filled with tears at the thought, tail sinking between her legs.

"I know you had bad experiences," he said patiently, giving her a kind pat on the head. "And I'm sorry for that. But this isn't working, you see? I only know how to take care of myself. And I can't give you what you need...or what you want." He was referring to the fire. She had started to pester him to light another one so that she could be warm, and they could be comfortable in the cabin. But the boy had decided against starting a fire ever again. His dreams were suddenly full of flames that licked his skin, hot and painful. Flames that consumed the home he had built, flames that destroyed all he had worked so hard for. And standing there, watching him in these dreams, was the fox.

"You're all I have," she said earnestly. "And I would rather be dead than without you." The words resounded with the boy, and he sighed as he realized that he was her oak. He was what she depended on most of all. He was the only thing that she was relying on, and he was beginning to realize what a burden that was becoming.

The fox demanded many things from him. He was expected to be near her always. He fed her, bathed her, kept her warm at night. She wanted him to care for her and only her. No longer was he allowed to feed his leftovers to the deer; his acts of charity made her wildly jealous. She refused to let him feed the birds, and even when he wanted to look out and watch the forest from his perch, she would complain.

"You can't leave me alone," she would say resolutely, and though the boy had fought against her control at first, he was beginning to weaken. It wasn't as though he thought of her as domineering. No, he pitied the fox. Pitied the way that she was alone, and he knew she had faced a painful past, being around those who she couldn't love. After all, she had almost died trying to run from them. There was a mantra that was beginning to echo in his head all the time now: "I'd rather be miserable and see her happy, than end it and see her miserable." And though it was true that he wanted for her to be happy—to have the lust for life she always had—it was becoming harder each day to deal with how tightly she clung to him.

It was a cool autumn morning when the boy and the fox went for a walk through the woods to forage. She had insisted on tagging along, as usual. And he had allowed it, knowing that it kept her from edging back into the dark place she went to when he suggested them going their separate ways. He and his companion walked to the water hole as they did each morning, and he was about to begin picking some ripened blueberries from the bush when he saw an animal that he didn't recognize. It was similar to a fox, though it was gray, and it looked more cat-like. It sipped gently from the water hole. For a moment, the boy observed it as it drank. He could feel the fox's eyes watching him as he looked at the animal.

"A lynx," she said, looking at the boy with a bored expression.

"He looks kind of like you," the boy said, raising his eyebrows. As though on cue, several other lynxes came out from the bush and joined the one that lapped at the water hole.

"A family of lynxes," said the fox, tilting her head. The boy could tell she was intrigued, perhaps also having the same thought he was. Though he doubted she was keen on leaving his side, he was ready to find another family for her. He approached the lynx family and addressed them.

"You have a beautiful family," he said, and the male looked up at him, appraising him coolly. There was something in the animal's eyes that made the boy feel uneasy. But he wanted to pass the fox off to a loving family, a family that would make her happy and keep her from that sadness she was so prone to.

"Thank you," the lynx said considering. He was the father, the boy could see that. There were three cubs, and a mother that was eyeing the fox with great interest. The fox didn't look impressed. "Your friend is quite beautiful," He looked at the fox as well, and he and the mother lynx exchanged glances. The boy wondered what they were thinking.

"We've been wanting another cub," said the mother, to the fox. "But no luck," She smiled. There was something about it that seemed disingenuous, but the boy didn't care. The fox needed a family, and what could be more perfect than this family of lynxes?

"She was orphaned," he blurted out, regretting his words when he saw the excited look on the lynx's faces.

"Poor dear," said the father, eyeing the fox. The boy didn't know what the look in his eyes was, but it made him very uncomfortable. "We always have room in our hollow. You should come live with us," He showed his teeth, and the boy found himself growing more and more uneasy. But he still wished for her to find a family, to be with someone who would love and care for her in a way he couldn't. Of course, he felt *something* for the fox; he cared enough for her that he was willing to put up with her need to control him. But ultimately, he needed to get his freedom back, and he didn't know how else to get it.

"You know," he began, turning to the fox. She eyed him with distaste. "It might be good for you to have a bigger family. Maybe this would be the perfect situation for you?"

"I want to stay with you," she hissed desperately, looking up at him with her wide eyes. The boy sighed and dropped to his knees, hugging the fox. Her claws immediately latched onto him, and he cried out in pain, pushing her off. She landed on the ground with a soft thud.

"We'll take her from here," The mother lynx said softly, picking the fox up by the scruff of her neck. The boy looked at the fox, and she gazed back, wordlessly. He could see, though, what her thoughts were as she stared him down. She was angry. Betrayed. Sad. He still, inexplicably, wanted to protect her, wanted to show her that he was there to keep her safe. But instead, he nodded and turned his back on the fox, quelling his doubts with the fierce joy of being free again.

For a whole season, he heard nothing from or about the fox. The boy happily went back to his life of solitude, enjoying his days in the sun and his evening whittling away. He enjoyed foraging when he wanted for the foods that he wanted, looking at the forest with nobody complaining, and nobody scratching him or scolding him. But he couldn't help but miss the little fox's presence. He knew in his heart that their life together had been difficult. It had in fact made him angry and miserable. She had tried so hard to take over every single aspect of his life, and now that she was gone, living with the lynx family, he had his freedom back.

But the look in her eyes when the lynx family took her haunted him. He thought of how sad she had seemed, and he recalled all of the times she had threatened to take her own life whenever he made any mention of being without her. His feelings confused him, and he wasn't sure what he truly wanted anymore. After all, the freedom he had craved was finally his once again. There were times in the evening when he would awaken with a sense of surprise that he didn't feel melancholic, but joyful, without the oppressive warmth of her small body beside his.

As time passed, however, and as winter gave way to spring, these doubts faded, and he came to terms with the fox being gone. His life had gone back to the simplistic joy that it had always been, and he found himself happily going through his days the same way he always had. The boy still thought of the fox often, and he hoped she was doing all right. He hoped that the lynx family treated her well and that she had found peace with them. Unfortunately, as he would soon realize, this was not the case.

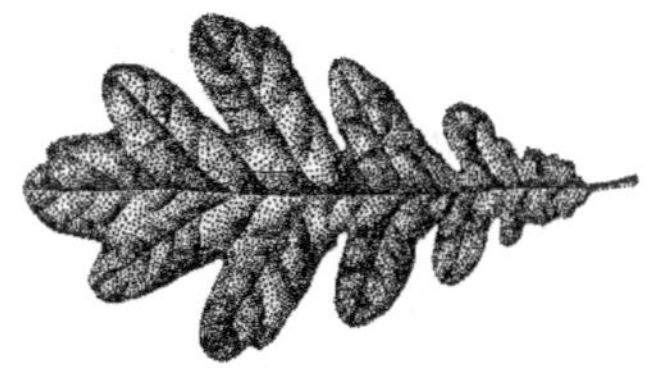

Spring came with more heavy rainfall, and the boy would enjoy the smell and sounds of these evenings, lying in bed as the rain pounded against the wooden roof of the cabin. He loved to let the rain lull him to sleep each night, and would smile as he breathed in the fresh air that came with the storms.

But one night, a strange sound intermingled with the rain. It was a familiar mewling, a crying, coming from down below the cabin. At first, as the boy lay awake in his bed, he did his best to ignore the sound. He didn't want to go out into the rain. But as the crying grew louder, the boy sighed and walked out of the cabin onto the branches. Looking down, he saw what he'd been afraid he'd find: the fox standing at the base of the oak, soaked in the downpour, sobbing. He didn't want to invite her in again. He didn't want to deal with her once more. But nonetheless, something within him couldn't leave her as he saw her there, so small and fragile. Sighing, he climbed down and wordlessly held her in his arms.

The boy brought the fox up to his cabin and dried her off, tending to the small wounds she had sustained while running through the forest. Brambles were caught in her fur, and she sniffled loudly, having caught a cold in the rain. As she thanked him and nuzzled into his chest once more, the boy thought that maybe, this time things would be different. Perhaps this time, she would be able to give him the freedom he wanted. At least, he wanted to think so.

And for a week, she was good to him. She allowed him to forage by himself. Allowed him to sculpt and whittle and carve. She didn't even complain when he ate a satchel's worth of hazelnuts. And during this week, the boy was full of hope. But that hope didn't last long.

Before long, the fox was back to her old ways. She was needy, desperate for his attention, and if she didn't get it, she would immediately threaten him that she would throw herself from the tree. One evening, she even did jump, landing hard on a branch and spraining her paw. It was a lucky thing that she survived, but the event gave the boy the resolution he needed to be rid of her once and for all. He could not let her run his life with threats of self-harm.

"I'm sorry," he said firmly as they stood outside of the cabin, at the base of the tree. Today was the day that he would take her to her own home, alone, and she lowered her head, seeming to know what he was going to say. "We both know this isn't healthy. I need to be alone. And really, I think you do, too." The boy knew it was for the better that they were separated. He was beginning to feel burdened by her. She clung to him so often that he couldn't continue to live that way. He wanted his home back to himself. He wanted his freedom, to be able to do as he pleased. He wanted to be able to have his time to think and dream and ponder. And he wanted to feel safe again; he did not want to live under the thumb of someone so volatile. "There's a hollow nearby, one that's been empty for a long while. It would be a beautiful place for you to start your own home. I think that it's time."

The fox didn't respond but looked up at him. He wasn't able to read her expression, though he was sure she wasn't happy. Anytime that he had suggested they part ways in the past had resulted in her lamenting that she wanted to die. But at least she wasn't doing that now, the boy thought to himself.

"I don't want to be away from you," she said finally, gazing at the cabin wistfully.

"I don't want you to stay here anymore," he said as kindly as possible. "I don't mean to be rude, but I miss my home being mine," She stared at him for a while, before giving a small nod. He smiled at her and led her towards the hollow.

When the boy arrived back at his home, he rejoiced in how empty it was without the fox. She would be fine, happy even, being away from him. Once she realized that it was better for her to be alone, better for her to be away from someone she felt the need to cling to, she would gain some clarity. This was all that the boy thought as he settled in for the evening.

But that night, he dreamt of the shadows of his past, for the first time in a long time. They felt closer now, as though they were a dark omen. The boy woke in a cold sweat as the sun was just beginning to rise.

As usual, the boy went out to forage for his breakfast. Things were normal; the sun shone prettily and created intricate patterns on the ground as he walked. He felt lighter. Happier. Until he smelled something all too familiar. Something that filled him with dread. The boy looked up at the sky and saw black smoke billowing up. With a sinking feeling, he ran back towards the oak tree, his heart pounding in his chest. It wasn't long before he realized that his beloved oak was engulfed in a fast-moving fire. A horrible, hungry fire that was beginning to consume everything in its path. It had already consumed the mighty tree and was beginning to spread everywhere, so much so that the boy knew he could never stop it, not with all the jugs of water in the world. Standing there, looking up at him with a scared expression on her face, was the fox. The boy looked at her full of pain, feeling his eyes welling up with tears as he felt the forest beginning to burn, fall to the ground in a pile of ash. He knew, somehow, that she had done this.

"I was just trying to come to see you," she said, her voice breaking. "I wanted to be warm. Wanted you to give me another chance,"

"You destroyed everything," he shook his head. "Since the day I met you, you've done nothing but hold me down and force things into my life! You controlled everything! You took so much from me. And now, you've even taken my home. I can't—I won't see you again," The fox sobbed as he spoke, but he could tell that she was pitying herself more than she felt for him. Truly, he realized in a flash of insight, she didn't care about his feelings at all. She had never cared about anything other than her own wants and desires.

And in a final act of selfishness, she had burned down his home. Whatever embers of affection remained within the boy for the fox died. He looked at her with ice in his gaze, and as he did so, her eyes widened, then closed. For the first time since he had met her, the fox seemed to genuinely realize what she had done. And while she might have still considered herself to be a victim in some sense, feeling as though he had abandoned her, perhaps she finally understood what she had done to him.

"I understand," she said, turning away. "I'll leave now." She trotted away, and the boy watched her go, rage and pain and fury all burned in his heart. It would be a long while before he healed from her. It would be a long while before the forest healed from her.

The boy turned and ran. Ran from the fire, from his home, from the only life he had ever known. And as he ran away from the fire, not know what would become of the fox or of the other animals of the forest, he tried to make sense of it all.

How could this happen? How could such a small thing, destroy so much? Why was it happening to him?

The boy collapsed to his knees, sobbing as he heard the crackling flames in the distance. He cried to himself, one phrase running through his mind: *I guess sometimes bad things happen to good people.*

When the fire eventually died, the once-thriving landscape was transformed. The vibrant forest was no more. Nothing remained but scorched earth, and as the boy walked back to the space where his oak had been, as he looked out onto the barren wasteland, he saw one thing. Hope. There was one thing in his satchel, and he pulled it out. A single acorn, sitting heavy in his palm. With a deep breath, and a single tear running down his cheek, the boy planted the acorn in the earth.

As time passed, the acorn became a small oak. A seedling that eventually grew large and strong, as did the other seedlings that the boy planted. And he grew as well, into a man who oversaw the forest and tended to it as carefully as he did his broken, hurting heart. He spent the rest of his days alone, watering the trees and watching as the animals tentatively made their way back to the forest.

It wasn't the same, but as time passed, it became home once more.

Author Bio

Joel E. Crosby was born in Germany and raised in the Netherlands, he was raised bilingual by an American father and a Dutch mother. He began writing before his age had double digits. When he's not writing, he can be found glued to his laptop thinking about writing, marketing, and developing new stories. Joel is the author of *The Boy and The Fox*, and currently lives in Zwolle, the Netherlands, with his wife.

You can connect with Joel on Facebook at facebook.com/JoelECrosby or on Instagram @Joel.Crosby. You can also visit his website, JoelCrosby.com, to sign up for emails about new releases.

facebook.com/JoelECrosby
instagram.com/Joel.Crosby